Thomas

Based on
The Railway Series
by the
Rev. W. Awdry

Illustrations by
Robin Davies

EGMONT

Thomas the Tank Engine **loved** working on his very own Branch Line.

Annie and Clarabel were Thomas' coaches. Annie could only take passengers, while Clarabel could take passengers, luggage and the Guard.

The coaches were old and needed new paint, but Thomas didn't mind. Annie and Clarabel were very special.

Thomas' favourite place along the line was the river. Each time he **rumbled** over the bridge, he would look out for people fishing.

Thomas often wished he could stay and watch.

"What would The Fat Controller say if we were late?" said his Driver.

Thomas still thought it would be fun to stop by the river one day, though.

When he met another engine he would say, "I want to go fishing."

But they all told him the same thing, "Engines don't go fishing!"

One day, Thomas stopped as usual to take on water at the station by the river.

But the water tower wasn't working.

"Bother!" said Thomas. "I'm thirsty."

"Never mind," said his Driver. "We'll get some water from the river."

Thomas' crew found a bucket and some rope and Thomas puffed back to the bridge.

The bucket was old and full of holes. The crew pulled up bucket after bucket and emptied water into Thomas' tank as quickly as they could.

SPLASH!

"That's better!" smiled Thomas. He puffed away with Annie and Clarabel rolling behind.

Suddenly, Thomas began to feel an ache in his boiler. Steam hissed from his safety valve, **"WHEEEESH!"**

"There's too much steam," said his Driver.

"Bust my buffers!" cried Thomas.

The crew dampened down his fire and Thomas struggled on.

"I'm going to burst," he said.

Thomas stopped just outside the last station and his crew uncoupled Annie and Clarabel. Then Thomas slid into a siding.

The Guard went to phone an Engine Inspector while the Driver found some signs. He put them in front of and behind Thomas.

DANGER KEEP AWAY, the signs said.

Soon, the Inspector and The Fat Controller arrived.

"Cheer up, Thomas," they said. "We'll soon put you right."

"The feed pipe is blocked," said the Inspector, checking Thomas. "I'll just look in the tanks."

He climbed up and peered inside.

DANGER
KEEP
AWAY

"Take a look at this, Sir!" said the Inspector.

So The Fat Controller clambered up. He looked inside and nearly fell off the ladder in surprise. "Inspector," he said, "there are **FISH** in the tank!"

"We must have fished them from the river with our bucket!" said Thomas.

"So Thomas, you have been fishing," said The Fat Controller. "We must get those fish out right away."

The crew all took turns at fishing in Thomas' tank, while The Fat Controller watched and shouted instructions.

Thomas felt very funny with the fish **wriggling** and **jiggling** in his tank.

When all the fish were caught, The Fat Controller, the Inspector and Thomas' crew had a lovely supper of fish and chips.

"That was delicious," The Fat Controller told Thomas. "But engines don't go fishing. You must promise not to do it again."

"I promise, Sir," said Thomas sadly. "Fishing is much too **wriggly!**"

Thomas' challenge to you

Look back through the pages of this book
and see if you can spot:

boat

rabbit

fish

fisherman

bucket